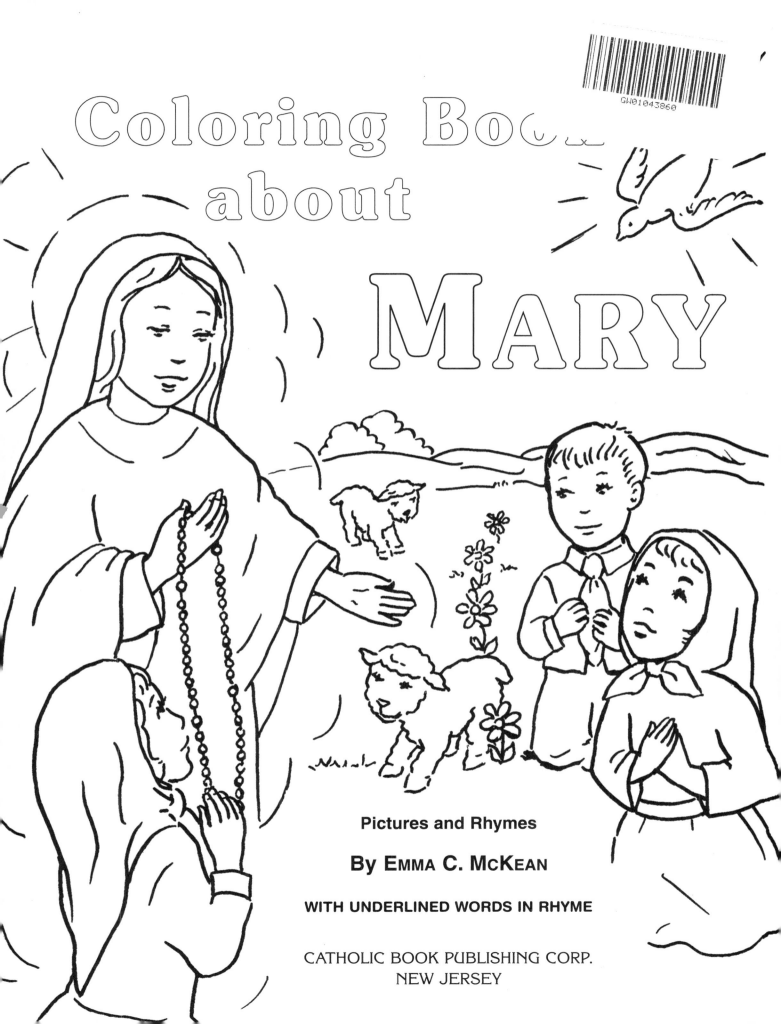

Coloring Book about MARY

Pictures and Rhymes

By Emma C. McKean

WITH UNDERLINED WORDS IN RHYME

CATHOLIC BOOK PUBLISHING CORP.
NEW JERSEY

MARY WITH HER MOTHER

So often when Mary
with her mother, Saint Anne,
Prayed to God in heaven
<u>above</u>,
They believed the LORD was
with them,
So great was their faith,
trust and
<u>love</u>.

(T-685)

NIHIL OBSTAT: Daniel V. Flynn, J.C.D., *Censor Librorum*
IMPRIMATUR: Patrick J. Sheridan, *Vicar General, Archdiocese of New York*

When Mary was a child in Nazareth,
   She learned from her mother, Saint <u>Anne</u>,
About the coming of the proclaimed Messiah,
   In God's Salvation <u>plan</u>.

When Mary grew up as the Blessed Virgin,
   She was greeted by an angel from the <u>LORD</u>,
Chosen was she to become Mother of JESUS,
   Through the Holy Spirit in heavenly <u>accord</u>.

THE BLESSED VIRGIN MARY WITH SAINT JOSEPH

The husband of Mary was Joseph,
A saintly carpenter, chosen to <u>be</u>
The foster father of JESUS
In the Holy Family of <u>three</u>.

MARY WITH ELIZABETH

When the Blessed Virgin visited her cousin,
The Holy Spirit let Elizabeth <u>know</u>
That Mary was to be the Mother of Jesus.
Mary's face had a shining <u>glow</u>.

MARY BECOMES THE MOTHER OF JESUS

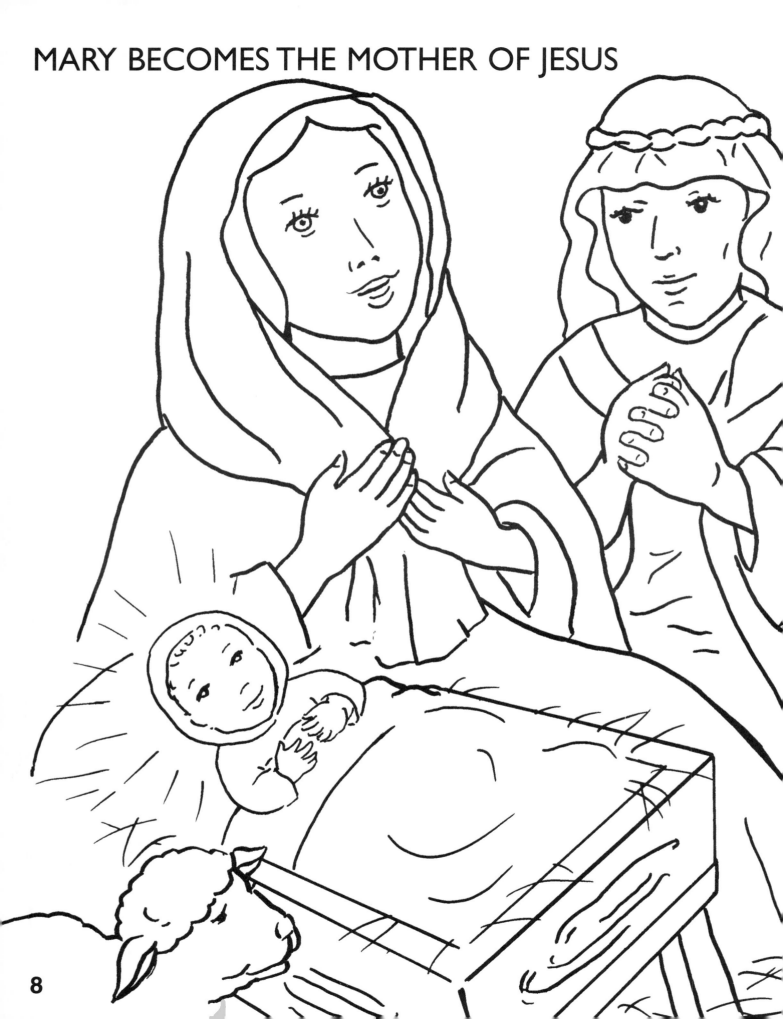

Shepherds told Mary,
An angel told <u>them</u>
The shepherds should go
To <u>Bethlehem.</u>

And when they got there,
They knelt down
<u>before</u>
The Little Lord Jesus
They came to <u>adore</u>.

When Mary presented Jesus
in the Temple,
Simeon knew the time was <u>right</u>,
To declare he saw OUR SAVIOR,
The long-awaited <u>LIGHT</u>!

This girl can see a picture,
She is thinking about <u>today</u>,
For the fourth decade
of the Rosary,
That she is going to <u>say</u>.

THE BLESSED VIRGIN MARY
PRESENTING JESUS
IN THE TEMPLE AT JERUSALEM

Simeon

The three Wise Men knelt
before Jesus,
Offering gifts they had
brought
with them . . .

12

As they gazed upon
    The Messiah,
With the Virgin
    in Bethle<u>hem</u>.

THE BLESSED VIRGIN MOTHER
MARY WITH HER
DIVINE SON JESUS

13

When Mary went looking for JESUS,
   This is what Mary <u>saw</u>:
Her twelve-year-old Son teaching
   The teachers of the <u>Law</u>!

MARY FINDS JESUS
IN THE TEMPLE

MARY ATTENDS A
MARRIAGE FEAST
AT CANA
IN GALILEE

One of the
waiters

So strong was Mary's faith in God—
  As a wedding guest she <u>knew</u>
Jesus could work a miracle, and
  At her request, He would <u>too</u>.

After jars were filled with water,
  The water was changed to <u>wine</u>,
People were amazed to see,
  This truly miraculous <u>sign</u>!

This boy is writing
the story,
About how Mary was
there to <u>see</u>,
Her precious Son,
Our Savior,
On the way
to <u>Calvary</u>.

MARY MEETS JESUS

Mary saw Jesus when He appeared
        to His disciples,
Forty days after He returned from the <u>dead</u>.
        On the Mount of Olives He blessed them,
        And rose into the clouds
                <u>overhead</u>.

The disciples returned to Jerusalem.
   Among them was Mary who <u>went</u>
To wait for the Holy Spirit
   That Jesus had said would be <u>sent</u>.

MARY
WATCHING
THE
ASCENSION

Mary was with the apostles,
When the Holy Spirit
came to <u>rest</u>,
Above the head of each
of them,
And Mary was especially
<u>blest</u>.

THE COMING
OF THE
HOLY SPIRIT
TO MARY
AND THE
APOSTLES

23

WE BELIEVE

The Blessed Virgin Mother Mary
Was taken up to heaven to <u>share</u>,
In the light of the Glory of JESUS.
She intercedes when we call her in <u>prayer</u>.

24

THE ASSUMPTION
OF THE BLESSED VIRGIN MARY

25

MARY, QUEEN OF THE MAY

These children with the maypole,
Have gathered here <u>today</u>,
To show their love
for Mary,
Who is
The Queen
of
<u>MAY</u>.

26

Thus—
To honor the Mother
  of JESUS,
  Our Heavenly Queen,
  they came,
And they paused
  to pray "Hail Mary,"
  And her goodness
  to proclaim.

THE LADY
OF THE
ROSARY

28

When the Lady appeared at Fatima
  She had a message to <u>convey</u>,
That the faithful "must say the Rosary," and
  "Ask pardon for their sins" when they <u>pray</u>.

When we say a "Hail Mary" together,
  As each holds a "Hail Mary" <u>bead</u>,
  We ask the Blessed Virgin Mary,
  To "Pray for us sinners,"
  That means—to <u>intercede</u>!

Marian hopes that many,
Throughout the world, may <u>heed</u>,
The call for prayer and penance,
For Mary to <u>intercede</u>.

THE HAIL MARY

These children are saying:
"Hail, Mary, full of grace! The Lord is with thee;
Blessed art thou among women,
And blessed is the fruit
of thy womb, JESUS.

Holy Mary, Mother
of God,
Pray for us sinners, now
And at the hour
of our death.
Amen."

Mary,
Blessed Virgin Mother of
Our Savior Jesus, <u>pray</u>,
That the virtues, faith and
trust and love,
May increase in us each <u>day</u>.